Here at Z & Z Toys Corp.,
We are determined to
transport you into a world
of active creative play. Our
Goofy Grin Monsters are
designed to be a positive
and fun part of your
learning experience.
We create the characters;
You create the adventures.

Library of Congress Cataloging-in-Publication Data

Mohammad, Zaid
Why Are There Monsters in My Rooom? / by Zaid Mohammad.
    p. cm.
ISBN 978-0-9889037-0-8
Library of Congress Control Number: 2013903016

Ordering information is available at:
www.goofygrinmonsters.com
or write to
customerservice@goofygrinmonsters.com.

To my daughter Sadia, the goofiest monster I know.

Goofy Grin Monsters WILL sneak into your room at night.

Not to scare you.

Not to frighten you.

Not to eat you.

Not to gobble you.

You know all the best game to play!

What is your favorite game to play?

Goofy Grin Monsters ARE
hiding under your bed.

Not to scare you.

Not to frighten you.

Not to eat you.

Not to gobble you.

They are playing Hide and Seek with you. "YOU'RE IT!"

What is your favorite hiding place when you play Hide and Seek?

Goofy Grin Monsters DO sneak out of your closet.

Not to scare you.

Not to frighten you.

Not to eat you.

Not to gobble you.

They are playing dress-up
with you.

What is your favorite
dress-up outfit?

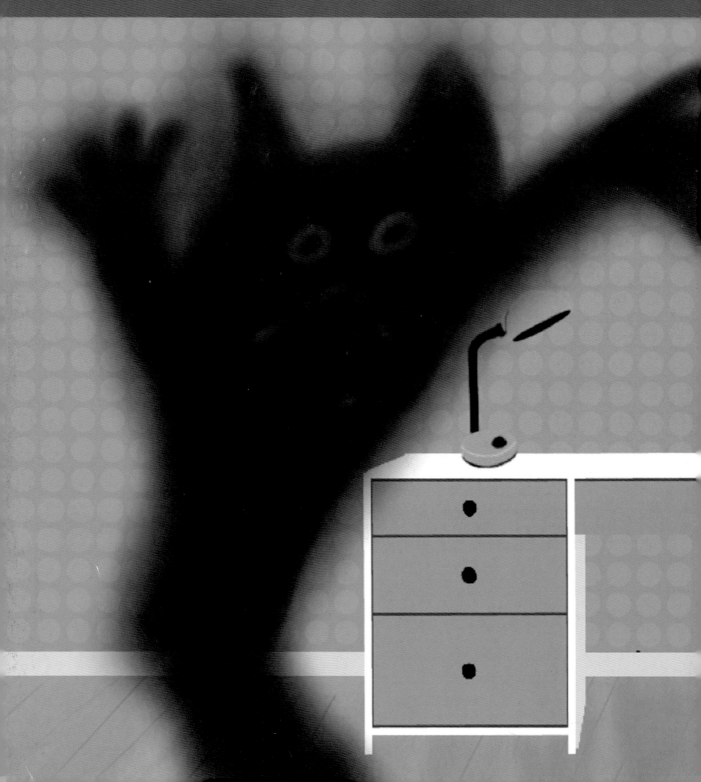

Goofy Grin Monsters MAY make shadows on your wall.

Not to scare you.

Not to frighten you.

Not to eat you.

Not to gobble you.

They are making shadow puppets with you.

Do you know how to make shadow puppets? What is your favorite kind?

Goofy Grin Monsters DO make dripping sounds in your bathroom.

Not to scare you.

Not to frighten you.

Not to eat you.

Not to gobble you.

They are just brushing their teeth with you.

Do you brush your teeth every night before you go to bed?

Not to scare you.

Not to frighten you.

Not to eat you.

Not to gobble you.

They scare away all the things that scare you!

What scares you at night?
The Goofy Grin Monsters
will keep you safe.

Goofy Grin Monsters WILL watch over you at night.

Not to scare you.

Not to frighten you.

Not to eat you.

Not to gobble you.

Unless they are too tired from a long day of playing, that is.

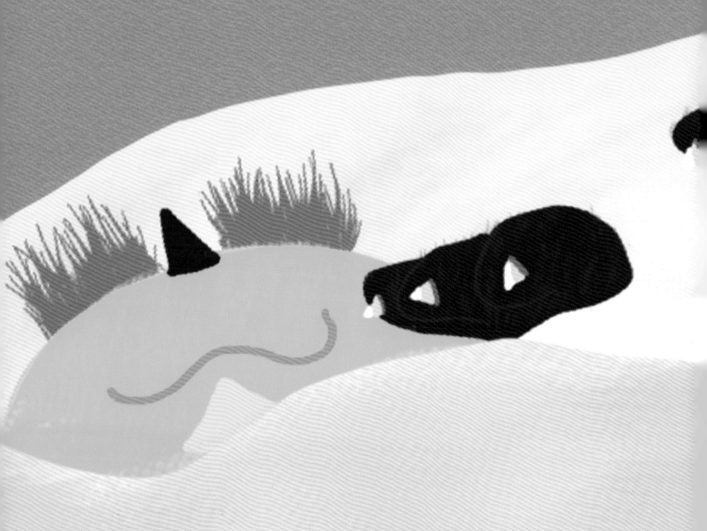

Do you get sleepy after you play all day? What time do you go to bed each night?

COMING SOON!

The Rise of Sloan

Writen By: Zaid Mohammad

Sweeter Candy

Writen By: Zaid Mohammad

Foggy Irmi

Writen By: Zaid Mohammad

The Birth of BoJoe

Writen By: Zaid Mohammad